WELCOME TO

Beast Quest

Collect the special coins in this book. You will earn one gold coin for every chapter you read.

Once you have finished all the chapters, find out what to do with your gold coins at the back of the book.

With special thanks to Michael Ford

To Kenny Heffernan – Ireland's biggest Beast Quest fan

www.beastquest.co.uk

ORCHARD BOOKS

First published in Great Britain in 2014 by The Watts Publishing Group
This edition published in 2018 by the Watts Publishing Group

1 3 5 7 9 10 8 6 4 2

Text © 2014 Beast Quest Limited.
Cover and inside illustrations by Steve Sims
© Beast Quest Limited 2014

Beast Quest is a registered trademark of Beast Quest Limited
Series created by Beast Quest Limited, London

A CIP catalogue record for this book is available from the British Library.

ISBN 978 1 40835 867 2

Printed and bound in Germany

The paper and board used in this book are made from wood from responsible sources

Orchard Books
An imprint of Hachette Children's Group
Part of The Watts Publishing Group Limited
Carmelite House, 50 Victoria Embankment, London EC4Y 0DZ

An Hachette UK Company
www.hachette.co.uk
www.hachettechildrens.co.uk

RAFFKOR
THE STAMPEDING
BRUTE

BY ADAM BLADE

ORCHARD

CONTENTS

Dear reader,

Do not pity me – my spells may be useless now, but my sixth sense will never go. Evil is afoot in this once peaceful kingdom. Jezrin the Judge may have been defeated by brave Tom, but his minions do not rest. Our many Quests have taught me that an enemy beaten back will return stronger than before.

Tonight I had a vision of the pale moon turning black. What it means is not clear, but a new menace stalks the land of Rion, and I fear it will spread to Avantia. My wizard instincts tell me that our enemies plan to tip the balance of nature, turning Good to Evil. A hero will be needed to stand against the dark forces. Can you guess who that hero might be?

Aduro, former wizard to King Hugo

PROLOGUE

Wilfred the Beast Keeper panted
hard as he took the final steps
towards the caves. The climb from
his hut down in the valley never got
any easier. Still, the safety of the
young Beasts was more important
than a few aches in his legs.

The entrance to the caves was
nearly invisible from the valley. Even
the people of Rion had no idea what

lived up here in the mountainside –
young Beasts in training. The Beasts
that would one day protect innocent
people in faraway kingdoms.

Entering the darkness of Raffkor's
cave, Wilfred expected to find the
young bull-Beast resting in his straw
– but there was no sign of him.

"Odd..." muttered Wilfred,
spying a trail of hoofprints leading
further into the depths of the cave.
"Raffkor!" he called. "Come on, you
lazy thing. We have training to be
getting on with."

But there was no sound. Worry
gnawed at Wilfred's mind. He hadn't
brought a torch – normally, the pale
blue glow that shone from Raffkor's
horns would have provided him with

enough light. The caves were pitch black today. He reached out blindly, using his hands to feel his way along the cold stone walls. He tripped, stumbling on the uneven ground.

There! A dim blue light seeped from the gloom ahead. From out of the gloom came a snort, and then a series of panicked low grunts.

"Raffkor?" Wilfred called, as he rounded a corner.

His feet skidded to a halt.

A tall woman stood in the centre of the cave, a cruel black whip raised above her head.

Wilfred recognised her wild hair and the gold and silver symbols stitched into her flowing robe.

"Kensa!" he gasped.

"Nice of you to join us," said the sorceress, smiling nastily.

Wilfred fumbled to draw his sword, but Kensa was too quick. With a flick of her wrist, the whip struck Wilfred's arm. He cried out in pain and the sword clattered to the ground. The sorceress lashed the whip across Raffkor's broad back. "Kill him!" she hissed.

The Beast moaned in pain and lowered his head to aim his four horns at Wilfred. Three of them glowed bright blue, while the fourth was blackened.

Wilfred dived aside as a bolt of blue light blasted from the Beast's horns. The Beast Keeper rolled across the rocky ground, scraping his knees and elbows, his foot twisting painfully. When he looked up, he saw the bolt had torn a gash on the cave wall right where he'd been standing.

The bull-Beast stamped forward, snorting loudly.

"Raffkor, please!" said Wilfred. Trying to stand, he felt a flash of pain in his ankle. "Remember who I am!"

He saw no recognition in the bull's eyes, only hatred. He was under Kensa's evil thrall. The blue energy was swirling through Raffkor's horns, building, building…

Wilfred cowered back against the cavern wall, which suddenly shook with a low rumble. Kensa's glance darted this way and that – she looked confused. With a crunch of

breaking stone, the far side of the cave collapsed in on itself. A green, glittering shape surged into the space and daylight flooded the darkness.

"Vedra!" Wilfred mumbled.

The green dragon swept over Wilfred, snatching him up with his talons and carrying him away, up the mountainside.

"Don't let them escape!" Kensa screeched shrilly.

Vedra twisted in the sky as a blue bolt shot from Raffkor's horns.

Wilfred felt the air around him burn as bright light forced his eyes closed. When he dared to open them again, the air was filled with smoke, and they were soaring high above the mountain top.

Raffkor and Kensa were lost beneath the clouds.

I'm alive, he thought with relief.

Vedra gave a keening cry as he lurched higher. Wilfred smelled burned flesh. With a sinking feeling, the Beast Keeper saw the deadly blast hadn't missed them completely. Across the dragon's green belly was a long, black scorch mark.

Vedra put his body in the way to save me, thought Wilfred. He looked down at the landscape flashing past. *What about the other young Beasts? Where are they?*

One thing was certain: Evil had come to Rion.

There was only one person who could help him now.

1

TOM'S REWARD

Storm lowered his head over the door of the stall as Tom fed him a tart green apple.

"There you go, boy," he said. "You deserve more than just a treat and new shoes, but that will have to do for now."

"It's good to be together again, isn't it?" said Elenna. She was sitting on a hay bale, tightening her bowstring. Silver lounged beside her.

Tom nodded. He had walked the Warrior's Road without his beloved steed, and had occasionally doubted they would ever be reunited.

He had only just triumphed on his last Quest.

A palace steward knocked at the stable door. "If you please, young sir and lady," he said. "His Majesty requests your presence in the banqueting hall."

"Of course!" said Elenna, leaping up. "I'd almost forgotten about dinner with King Hugo."

Tom ruffled Storm's mane and they followed the steward to the palace.

When the steward threw open the tall wooden doors, Tom gasped. He'd expected just King Hugo, Wizard Daltec, and Aduro, but the hall was packed with people. Courtiers, servants and soldiers filled the benches. Candles blazed in their holders and the tables groaned under the weight of platters of roasted meats, wheels of cheese and piles of fruit.

King Hugo stood up, raising a goblet. The room burst into wild applause. Flushing with embarrassment, Tom whispered, "Is this all for us?"

Elenna's eyes were wide. "It looks like it," she said.

"Let the festivities begin!" cried King Hugo, gesturing to the empty seats either side of him.

Tom and Elenna made their way through the crowd, as people patted them on the back. Even Captain Harkman managed a smile, though it looked a little like a grimace.

"Good to have you home, Tom," he said gruffly.

Tom settled into the seat beside the king, and lowered his voice.

"This isn't all for me and Elenna, surely?" he asked. "The people of Avantia aren't supposed to know about the Beasts."

King Hugo grinned. "It's a double celebration," he said. "Your successful Quest, as well as the anniversary of my coronation."

Aduro smiled, rose from his seat and lifted his goblet. "A toast!" the former wizard declared. "To King Hugo's many years on the throne, and to many more!"

Tom and Elenna raised cups of fruit juice and joined in with the chorus.

"To King Hugo!"

Time seemed to fly past. Tom ate until his stomach felt close to bursting. Elenna passed scraps of meat beneath the table to Silver. As the platters were being cleared away, the music grew louder, drowning out the voices of the feasters. Tumblers and acrobats began to perform in front of the weary guests.

King Hugo had already retired to

bed and Tom's eyelids were starting
to droop as he watched a fire-
breather. *I can't remember the last
time I felt this tired*, he thought.
Then he noticed that Daltec was
beckoning to him from the far side of

the room. *What can he want?*

Tom nudged Elenna. "Something's wrong. Let's find out what."

Silver yawned and got up, leaving the bone he'd been gnawing. Tom led the way towards the young wizard.

"Is it Jezrin the Judge?" Tom asked. Their enemy had vanished when they returned from the Warrior's Road, his evil plans defeated. "Has there been any news of him?"

"We've heard nothing," said Daltec, shaking his head. "The Circle of Wizards has banished him from their number. Aduro believes it will be some time before he regains enough strength to attack the kingdom again."

"Then what's wrong?" Elenna asked, looking at him worriedly.

Daltec's face was grave. "You had better follow me."

He led them through a side door and along a narrow, unlit corridor. The air was cool after the crowded banqueting hall, and the sounds of the celebration grew muted.

They reached the end of the passage, and Daltec drew aside a heavy curtain. On the other side was a small chamber lit by a fire burning in the hearth. King Hugo sat in a chair in the centre of the room. *So he's not in bed, after all!* Aduro stood leaning on a staff at his side.

The king stood up. "I have a mission for you both," he said.

"A new Quest?" asked Tom, feeling a rush of anticipation. If a new threat had reached Avantia's shores, he was ready to face it.

"Something tells me that this Quest will be the hardest you have undertaken," Aduro added.

Tom sensed Elenna stiffen beside him. "Tell us," he said.

The king looked Tom straight in the eye. "You will go on an epic Quest" – his face split into a grin – "to Errinel, where you will visit your aunt and uncle, and get some rest."

Tom frowned. "Rest?" he repeated. "What do you mean?"

The king placed both hands on Tom's shoulders. "You've defended Avantia from many enemies. It's time for you to stop looking for danger around every corner. You've earned a break."

"But…" Tom began. He caught a glimpse of Elenna grinning from the corner of his eye.

"That's an order," said King Hugo. "You would not disobey your king, would you?"

Tom sighed. "No, Your Majesty," he said, and a fresh wave of weariness washed over him.

Perhaps a rest would be good...

For the first time in ages, Tom would see his relatives again – and have nothing to do but eat cherry pie!

2

AN UNEXPECTED ARRIVAL

Tom woke feeling warm and snug on a feather-stuffed mattress. Morning light crept in between a crack in the shutters. Panic surged through his chest. He quickly threw off the blanket, looking for his sword and shield. *Then he remembered: I don't have to get up. There is no Quest...*

His beating heart slowing, he

crossed to the windows and opened the shutters. The sun was already high above the castle walls.

I haven't had a lie-in for so long, Tom thought. *Oh well, I'm following the king's orders.*

He washed and dressed, and headed down to the palace courtyard. Servants scurried about, preparing for the second day of the coronation celebrations. Some were hanging bunting over the main gate, others were carrying wood to make a bonfire. Tom found Elenna eating a plate of cheese outside the stables. She started laughing.

Tom frowned. "What's so funny?"

"Have you seen your hair this morning?" she asked.

Tom walked over to a water trough and stared at his reflection. His thick brown hair was sticking up in all directions. Grinning, he scooped a handful of cold water over his head to smooth it down, then turned to his friend.

"Ready to go?" he asked. They'd planned the night before to head out together to Tom's village, Errinel. After that, Elenna would journey to the western coast to visit her fisherman uncle.

"Silver and I have been ready since dawn," she said, offering him the rest of her breakfast. "Here, you should eat before we set out."

Tom's stomach was rumbling, but he didn't want to delay any more.

"I'm sure Aunt Maria will have baked," he said. "I can wait!"

After he'd saddled Storm, Elenna mounted behind him and they trotted out towards the gates.

Stands were being set up for a joust that would take place later that evening. As Storm clopped across the courtyard, Aduro shambled from the palace. He walked quickly, muttering to himself. Tom slowed his stallion and watched as the old wizard made his way towards a low arched doorway.

The Secret Library, Tom thought. *I wonder why he's going in there.*

"Aduro!" Tom called.

His friend stopped in his tracks and spun round.

"Greetings," he said, quickly
smiling. "I thought you would have
left already."

The wizard's smile didn't fool Tom.
He could see the worry in Aduro's eyes.

"Is everything all right?" he asked.

"Oh, yes," said Aduro, throwing
a glance at the library door. "Quite

all right. You two must be off. Enjoy yourselves." Without waiting for a reply, he ducked under the arch and vanished down the library steps.

"He's acting oddly," Tom said to Elenna. "Should we follow him?"

"You heard what he said," replied Elenna. "There's nothing to worry about. He's probably just researching some ancient spell books!"

Tom pushed his dark thoughts aside and gave Storm's flanks a nudge. "You're right. Let's get going – otherwise it'll be dark before we reach Errinel."

"And, more importantly," said Elenna, "your uncle might have eaten all the cherry pie!"

Captain Harkman stood over the

gate-tower, and gave Tom a wave.

"It's all right for some," he called down. "I don't get a day off!" He pointed to a soldier manning the battlements. "Nor do you. Stop slouching!"

Both Tom and Elenna laughed as Storm crossed the drawbridge out into the fields beyond.

The sun had risen to its peak, warming Tom's back as they galloped down the dusty road that led out of the City. Silver kept pace beside them, his tongue lolling. Other travellers on the road waved and watched them fly past. The crops in the fields were almost ready to harvest. Golden ears of corn fluttered in the light breeze. Tom's heart surged to see the kingdom at peace after so many Quests. With their enemies defeated and evil at bay, balance had returned to Avantia.

A sudden shadow fell over them. Tom glanced up, and his breath caught in his throat as he reined Storm to a halt. Something dark was passing behind the pale clouds ahead – something quick and huge. Silver was growling, pawing at the earth.

"What in all Avantia?" muttered Elenna, looking at it.

Storm tossed his head, nostrils flaring. Tom smelled it too – sulphur.

"A dragon!" he said, sliding from Storm's back and drawing his sword.

A new enemy...

But as a green, scaled body broke through the clouds, Tom realised this was no foe, but a friend. "It's Vedra!"

The dragon had grown even more since Tom last saw him in Rion. He was almost the size of Ferno now. His mighty wings heaved up and down, but not fast enough to stop him falling. Something was wrong.

Tom watched as the dragon slid out of the sky, straining to keep his head aloft. Across his belly was a black scar, like a burn. A figure crouched low against his back.

"He's going to crash!" said Elenna.

With a moan, Vedra slammed into the ground, throwing up clods of soil and making the earth rumble. The

figure on Vedra's back somersaulted
across the field, sprawling into the
long grass with a cry. Tom recognised
him at once.

"That's Wilfred!" he exclaimed.
"The Beast Keeper of Rion."

3

THE WOUNDED DRAGON

Tom rushed to Wilfred's side. The Beast Keeper was sitting up, rubbing his head. His face was gaunt, his hair windswept. Tom saw blisters on his hands and realised he must have been gripping Vedra's scales for dear life on the perilous flight from Rion.

"Great danger..." mumbled Wilfred. "Beasts cursed... Evil..."

"Shhh, quiet for now," said Elenna calmly, arriving at Tom's side. "Just be still, Wilfred."

She cushioned his head in her hands and helped him to lie back.

Vedra let out a pained hiss from a few paces away. He tried to lift his neck, but it sagged back onto the ground. One wing flapped weakly, the other was folded beneath his body. It might have been broken.

Tom looked around desperately. He had to get the dragon to safety, but the crash would have been heard for miles. He could not let the people of Avantia know about the existence of the Beasts.

"Other travellers will pass this way," he said. "We need to hide Vedra."

Elenna looked aghast. "But how?
We can't possibly move a dragon!"

The air sizzled and in a puff of
smoke, Daltec appeared beside them.
"I saw what happened in my crystal
ball," said the young wizard.

"Can you magic Vedra back to the palace?" asked Tom.

Daltec shook his head. "Even when Aduro still had his magic, he would have struggled to move such a big Beast," he said. "The king is sending a platoon of his strongest troops, with horses and a cart to draw Vedra to the palace."

Muttering a spell, he pointed at the dragon. Blue light swirled from his fingertips, wrapping itself around Vedra's body. When the light cleared, an enormous cart had appeared beneath the Good Beast.

Vedra's flanks rose and fell quickly, as if he was struggling to breathe. Daltec frowned. "Now, let me think... how does it go?" He pointed again.

*"Clouds and cloaks, shadows and
    lies,
Hide this creature from human
    eyes."*

A velvet blanket appeared in the
air and draped itself over the Beast.
The cart and the dragon vanished.

"We need to be quick," said Daltec.
"The concealment spell won't
last for long." He crouched beside
Wilfrcd, placing a hand on the
Beast Keeper's head and muttering
another spell.

With a gasp, Wilfred opened his
eyes and struggled into a sitting
position. He stared straight at Tom.
"Terrible Evil," he said. "I had to
come and warn you. Avantia is in
great danger!"

Night had fallen over the City, and all the celebrations had been cancelled. The guests had been told that King Hugo was ill, but the truth was far worse. The king sat with his head resting on his hands in the cellar beneath the palace. Vedra lay curled in the centre of the room, sleeping fitfully. Despite the late hour and the long march back to the palace with the hidden cart, Tom was wide awake. Daltec and Aduro had been talking to Wilfred for some time, looking closely at the black burn on Vedra's belly.

Is it my imagination, Tom wondered, *or is the wound growing?*

"Well, Daltec?" asked the king.

"Your Majesty, it's not good."

Tom swallowed. "Will Vedra die?"

"Worse," said Daltec. "The green dragon has been poisoned with lunar blood. Evil is spreading through his veins as we speak. By the next full moon, the transformation will be complete – Vedra's scales will turn black and he will no longer be a Good Beast."

Aduro looked cross with himself. "I sensed trouble brewing," he mumbled. "That's why I was in the library poring over ancient scrolls. I should have acted…"

Tom's fists clenched at his sides. "There must be something we can do to save him." He remembered the day the twin dragons had hatched – how he'd kept them safe from harm. *There's no way I'm giving up on Vedra now!*

Aduro clutched a sheaf of old parchment to his chest. "There is one cure...but it means completing a dangerous Quest."

Tom gripped his sword hilt. "Then we'll leave at once."

Aduro held up his hand. "The old books say there's only one remedy for the Evil that infects Vedra – the Gilded Elixir. Its four ingredients are found in the four corners of the kingdom. You must travel far, and quickly, if you're to gather them in time."

"Storm is already saddled," said Tom, walking towards the door. "Do you have a map for me?"

Aduro nodded, and held up the parchment in his hand. "It's not as simple as finding the ingredients," said the former wizard. "Kensa will certainly have laid traps in your way."

"Kensa the Sorceress!" said Tom. "So she's behind this?"

"That's right," said Aduro. "With Jezrin the Judge gone, I knew it would not be long before she started causing her own trouble, but I didn't think she would act so quickly." He lowered his head towards King Hugo. "I should have warned you sooner, Your Majesty."

"We must all be wary," said the king. "Evil never rests."

Wilfred was wringing his hands. "I tried to stop her," he said, "but she had already turned Raffkor to Evil. Poor Vedra was wounded trying to save me."

Elenna rested a comforting hand on the Beast Keeper's shoulder. "You couldn't have known Kensa's plans. Don't worry, we will stop her."

Tom looked at his friend. "That's right. But time is precious – and we've wasted enough already. Let's go!"

4

A NEW QUEST

Aduro spread out an old map on a
table. "I found this in the library
as well, tucked into the back of an
ancient book." He pointed to the four
corners in turn. "Your first destination
is the Northern Mountains. From
there you'll head south to the Ruby
Desert, then east to the Dark Jungle.
The last journey will be north again –
to the Pit of Fire."

Tom added up the vast distances in his head. *We won't have time to cover that much ground before the next full moon...*

From Elenna's creased forehead, he guessed that she was thinking the same thing.

"You haven't told him about the others?" said Wilfred from the corner of the room.

"Others?" said Elenna.

Daltec shared a glance with Aduro. "The other Beasts of Rion," said the young wizard. "We don't know what has happened to them. My crystal ball is blank. It's likely they, too, are under Kensa's spells."

"Raffkor didn't recognise me at all," said Wilfred. "He attacked me!"

Tom recalled the brave young bull-Beast from his last visit to Rion. Then, Raffkor had been stubborn, but good at heart. *If he's turned Evil, then this Quest will be even harder.* "What about Falra?" Tom asked. "And Vislak? And Tikron? Surely they can't all be cursed?"

"I'm afraid it looks that way," said Aduro. "Kensa will use every weapon she has against you. Which means that you will be fighting Beasts who were once your allies."

Tom felt his hopes fading, but he tapped his shield. "At least I can summon the other Good Beasts to help me."

Aduro shook his head. "If Kensa has magic to corrupt Good Beasts, it's too risky – she might be able to turn more of them to Evil. It would stack the odds even higher against you. No, I'm afraid you two must tackle this Quest alone."

"Not alone," said Wilfred, quickly. He squared his shoulders. "I'm coming too. It's my duty to protect these Beasts."

Tom looked at the young man doubtfully. "Kensa and Sanpao will have no mercy," he said. "You'll be safer here."

Wilfred's face fell.

"You will not be facing Sanpao this time," said Daltec.

"What do you mean?" asked Elenna. "Wherever Kensa goes, the pirate king is never far behind."

"Since you left to walk the
Warrior's Road, he and Kensa
have fallen out," said Daltec. "The
sorceress is now working alone."

Tom folded the map and tucked
it into his tunic. Daltec held out a

leather sack, studded with iron and stitched with silver thread.

"Place the ingredients in this," he said. "The first one you will need to find is starleaf. It grows only on the Murmuring Peak – one of the tallest of the Northern Mountains."

As he and Elenna rushed to the stables, Tom felt like a fool. *To think I was going to go to Errinel. I should have realised something was wrong.*

Storm whinnied impatiently. *He senses the danger too,* thought Tom.

As Tom swung himself into the saddle, Wilfred came running into the courtyard after him. He wore a travelling cloak. "Don't try to talk me out of it," he said. "I'm coming with you both."

Perhaps I was wrong about the Beast Keeper, thought Tom. He sensed a steely fighting spirit beneath Wilfred's pale skin. After all, hadn't the young man ridden a dragon all the way to Avantia from Rion?

"You'll find Breeze in there," Tom said, nodding towards the stables. "Saddle her up. We ride at once!"

5

RETURN TO THE NORTH

Tom rode half-asleep, lulled by the rhythmic drumming of the horses' cantering hooves. He felt Elenna's grip on his waist tighten.

"We're almost there," she muttered.

Tom looked up to see the glorious peaks of the Northern Mountains silhouetted against the dawn light. His fingers were cramping on the reins. They had ridden for two nights, only stopping so the horses could drink from streams. Even Silver looked weary after the long slog across fields and farms and open plains. Each time Tom had been tempted to stop, he had imagined Kensa's grinning face and it had driven him on. *How could she poison the hearts of innocent young Beasts?*

Colour seeped into the mountains as the sun rose higher. Tom felt a shudder of recognition. One of his first Quests had brought him here – to free Arcta the Mountain Giant from Malvel's Evil enchantment.

Tom urged Storm up the narrow, dusty paths. Wilfred came behind on Breeze. The Beast Keeper clutched the horse's neck in panic – he was not a natural rider.

"Keep an eye out for Kensa," Tom told them.

The first village they came to made Tom's blood run cold. The simple stone buildings lay in ruins, crushed under boulders that had tumbled from above. There were no people in sight.

"Has there been an earthquake?" asked Elenna.

"Only a Beast could cause such a powerful tremor," said Tom.

"Raffkor," whispered Wilfred. "He used to love causing landslides when he was untrained and mischievous. I managed to channel his anger, but Kensa must be using it for Evil."

The next settlement was the same,

and so was the next – just deserted, collapsed homes, half-buried under rubble. Tom saw a child's wooden soldier puppet lying broken on the ground. His heart hardened. *I can't let these people down*, he thought.

As they picked their way through the debris, a distant tremor shook the ground, and more stones rattled down. "We're getting closer," said Tom. He wasn't sure how he felt about facing Raffkor. *Can I find it in my heart to fight a friend?*

Human voices interrupted his thoughts and Tom quickly slid off Storm's back, running in a crouch to a low rise ahead. He peered over the top as Elenna and Wilfred joined him.

A group of men and women were carrying makeshift picks, axes and staffs as they climbed the mountain slope. The ground was rough, with shallow ravines filled with strewn boulders. The group had a pack of dogs with them, straining at their leashes. Their clothes were torn and dirty. *They must be from the abandoned villages,* Tom thought.

"Are you sure it's this way, Ched?" asked a woman.

The bearded man who was leading the group shot her an angry look. "The dogs can smell something, Selima," he said. "When we find what's causing the rockfalls, we can kill it – then our misery will be over."

"But how can you be sure there's something up there?" asked Selima.

Ched stared up the mountain. "There's nothing natural about these landslides," he said. "They happen when the weather is calm. And you've heard the strange bellowing – and the roars."

At that very moment, the red jewel in Tom's belt began to glow, and a frightened message crept into his head.

People come. People angry.

Tom recognised the voice as Arcta's.

Wilfred made to stand, but Tom pulled him back.

"Wait!" he said.

"But they'll kill Raffkor," said the Beast Keeper. "Or he'll kill them!"

"No, they won't," said Tom, pulling out his map. "If I'm right, it's another scent those dogs are following."
He showed the map to Elenna, and pointed at a spot between two looming peaks. "Do you remember this place?"

Elenna's eyes widened. "Arcta's lair!"

Tom nodded grimly. "Arcta's a friendly Beast, but if these mountain folk attack him, he'll defend himself.

We have to stop them, but there are only three of us. We have to be clever."

People close, came Arcta's voice.

Tom scanned the horizon and – *There he is!* – the mountain giant's shaggy head was peering above a ridge. The villagers were heading right for him!

Tom touched the red jewel and sent a warning to his friend: *Stay completely out of sight.*

Arcta dipped behind the ridge again, but Tom could sense his fear and confusion. He needed a better plan. He had to keep Arcta calm and stop the villagers before they reached the Beast's lair.

"I've got it," he said, slipping his shield off his shoulder. "Wilfred, take this." He removed the feather from his shield — the token he'd won from Arcta when they had first faced one another.

He handed it to the Beast Keeper.

Wilfred frowned. "What am I supposed to do with this?"

Tom traced a loop on the map.

"Ride ahead, around the search party. Go to Arcta." Wilfred went white. "Don't worry," said Tom. "This feather will tell him you can be trusted. He'll realise I must have given it to you. I want you to try and keep him from breaking cover. Reassure him."

"What if he doesn't understand me?" said Wilfred.

Tom frowned. "Hopefully the feather will be enough. If not, you must have gestures you use when training Beasts."

"They work on young Beasts, yes," said Wilfred. "Arcta's fully grown!"

"You can do it," said Elenna. "We believe in you."

Wilfred took the feather, and

climbed back onto Breeze. "I won't let you down."

He set off at a canter and soon disappeared over a rocky shelf, along a sunken path, staying out of sight of the search party.

"And what are you going to do?" Elenna asked Tom.

"Cause a distraction," Tom replied.

He set off at a run, darting between boulders to avoid being seen. He was breathing hard by the time he reached the place he'd spotted, which was scattered with more rocks.

The searchers had almost reached the area where Arcta was hiding. There wasn't much time. *I just hope that Wilfred can convince Arcta to stay put!*

6

A VILLAGE IN FEAR

Tom drew his sword, and buried its point beneath a boulder the size of a barrel. He heaved, trying to lever the boulder down the slope. It didn't budge. *I have to try harder.*

Summoning the power of his golden breastplate, he pushed again. Magical strength flowed through his arms and the boulder tipped, beginning to roll down the slope. As it bounced along, it smashed more rocks, creating a hail of earth and stone.

Tom saw the party of villagers stop and look back. The rockfall had missed them by a hundred paces, just as Tom had planned. He waited, hoping they would turn back to investigate the landslide. But the dogs were still nosing the other way – towards Arcta.

Tom held his breath.

"The creature must have circled behind us," the leader called, pointing towards the settling dust. He began hurrying towards it, his companions following.

Tom let out a sigh of relief, and hurried back to Elenna.

"You did it!" she said with a grin.

But Tom couldn't bring himself to smile. "We've lost precious time already," he said, pointing along a path that led eastwards towards a sharp peak. "The map says the starleaf is that way."

Ched and the villagers had disappeared over a ridge of the mountain, so Tom and Elenna set off with the animals, back along the path.

Soon they reached another settlement, directly on their route. Tom's spirits lifted a little when he saw it was intact. Smoke rose from chimneys and people milled around the houses and market stalls.

"At least Raffkor's havoc hasn't reached this far," he said to Elenna.

As Tom climbed off Storm to lead
him through the market, Silver
growled in warning.

Tom spun around, and saw the
villagers had all stopped dead,
watching Tom and Elenna with
cold eyes.

"We don't welcome looters here,"

said a young woman loudly.

More of the crowd edged closer.
Some were snatching up weapons.

"We've had enough of your sort,"
said a grizzled man with muscular
arms. "Just because your village has
been destroyed, don't think that
you're welcome in ours."

"Tom!" hissed Elenna.

He turned and saw the search party from the mountain, their faces twisted with hate. The dogs were drooling, baring their teeth. *This must be their village!*

"What have we got here?" said the leader, Ched, in a low, menacing voice.

He didn't look happy to see them.

Tom resisted the urge to reach for his sword. "We're not looters!" he said, as Silver snapped his head back and forth.

"The boy's got a blade, Ched," said the woman sharply. "And the girl's got a bow."

The bearded man stepped forward. "Why do you carry weapons?"

"We..." Tom couldn't think of anything to say. He couldn't tell them the truth, about the Beasts and their Quest. "We're here on the king's business," he said at last.

The villager narrowed his eyes. "And what business is that?"

Tom could feel the suspicion growing from every side. "King Hugo has asked us..." He paused, searching for a reason. "He has asked us..."

The crowd pressed closer.

"We're here to investigate the rockfalls," said Elenna. "The king takes his subjects' plight very seriously indeed."

There were mutterings of approval from the villagers. "About time the king sent someone," said Selima.

"We've seen the other villages affected," added Tom. "It's terrible to behold."

Many lowered their weapons, including Ched.

"Then you're welcome here," he said. "Ask whatever you require, and we will do our best to help you. We've heard strange sounds echoing in the mountains – like an animal in a rage."

Tom kept his features calm. The last thing he wanted was for the villagers to know what was actually making the noises.

"The wind makes odd sounds sometimes," he said.

Ched shrugged. "Not like this. We fear our village will be next," he said.

Tom clapped him on the arm. "Don't worry, I assure you," he said. "We're here now."

"Before you continue," said the leader, "you must have a nice cool drink to prepare you for your climb. Follow me."

Tom felt a twinge of frustration. Every moment was precious on this Quest to find the starleaf.

"Be patient," whispered Elenna, obviously sensing his thoughts. "We mustn't blow our cover."

Ched led them through the market, to a stall with a painted sign showing oranges.

"Freshly squeezed juice," rasped a woman in a thick hooded shawl and long cloak. Tom couldn't see her face, but she sounded elderly.

He wasn't thirsty, but Elenna was right – they had an act to keep up.

"Two cups, please," he said, moving closer. Storm strained against the reins slightly. "We'll be on our way soon," he told his horse.

The old woman dropped an armful of oranges into a strange device shaped like a cylinder. She turned a handle and juice dribbled from a spout into a waiting cup. "You'll never forget Asnek's juice," she said, still winding the handle.

Silver paced back and forth. *He doesn't like all these people around him*, thought Tom.

The cloaked stallholder filled one cup and placed another under the spout. She handed Tom and Elenna a cup each. Tom noticed that her hands were unwrinkled. *Perhaps she isn't as old as she sounds.*

"How much do we owe you?" Elenna asked.

The woman waved dismissively. "For two servants of the king? Nothing! It's my pleasure!"

"Thank you," said Tom.

Silver leaped up, placing his front paws on the table and sending oranges scattering onto the ground.

"Silver, no!" said Elenna, pushing him back and apologising to the stallholder. "I don't know what's got into him."

"No matter," said the woman. "Tell me, do you expect to return from your investigation in the mountains?"

What a strange question, Tom thought. "I hope so. Here's to a successful mission," he said, raising his cup of delicious-smelling juice.

Elenna touched her cup to his. But as she went to take a drink, Silver yelped and jumped up again, and nipped her arm.

"Ouch!" she said. The cup fell from her hand. "Silver, whatever is the matt—"

Smoke rose from the ground, making a hissing noise as the rock at Elenna's feet melted where the juice had spilled.

"Acid!" Tom gasped.

7

FIGHTING AN OLD ENEMY

Tom threw his cup aside, drawing his sword and pointing the tip of the blade at the cloaked figure.

"Who are you?" he demanded.

The woman straightened up, rising a head taller than Tom, and pulled back her hood, revealing wild hair and a cruel, narrow face. The figure threw off her cloak to show a black velvet robe marked with strange symbols and lightning bolts. Her walking stick magically grew into a carved silver staff.

The villagers gasped and drew back.

"How nice to see you again," said Kensa. "Now prepare to die!"

With a flick of her staff, the table tipped and the cup of acid flew towards Tom's head. He ducked and the liquid shot past his face, hissing as it splashed to the ground behind him. Tom turned to make sure no one else was hurt, then felt Kensa's foot catch him in the stomach and send him sprawling across the ground. His sword flew from his grasp and his head slammed against a rock.

Through blurred vision, Tom saw

Kensa stoop to snatch up his sword, then pounce forward, slicing it at him. Tom rolled, hearing the steel bite into rock and villagers cry out as they scattered to safety.

Tom sprang to his feet as Kensa rushed at him, her staff and Tom's sword cutting rapid arcs. Tom used both hands to grip his shield as the blows slammed into him. He'd fought many skilled warriors in his time, but facing Kensa was like tackling three fighters at once. Silver growled and paced closer, but Tom's flashing blade drove him back to Elenna's side.

As Tom spun to avoid being cut in two by his own sword, he caught a glimpse of Elenna. She had an arrow to her bowstring. "I can't get a clear shot!" she cried.

Tom knew that he and Kensa were moving around too quickly for Elenna to dare fire an arrow. If she missed Kensa, she'd hit an innocent villager.

"Throw me your bow!" Tom cried.

Elenna tossed it to him. Kensa jabbed with Tom's sword, and he sidestepped to catch the bow. He felt the power of the amber jewel in his belt, making him move lightning-fast to slip the bow under Kensa's guard and jab her hard in the ribs. The sorceress doubled up, gasping for breath. Tom swung his weapon and smashed it into Kensa's legs, knocking her feet from beneath her. Kensa landed on her back with a cry. Leaping forward, Tom stepped on her wrist, pinning her sword-arm to the ground. Silver pounced onto her other arm, so she couldn't use her staff either.

"It's over," said Tom, pressing the

bow-tip against the witch's throat.

She squirmed, then fell back with a grimace.

"All right," she said weakly. "You win."

Tom handed the bow back to Elenna and bent over to reclaim his sword.

Oof!

Kensa twisted free and kicked Tom in the thigh. He fell to one knee as pain shot up his leg. Kensa's other foot caught Silver in the middle, and the wolf rolled over, yelping. In the blink of an eye, Kensa was on her feet and sprinting through the crowd.

"Out of my way, bumpkins!" she cried, swiping with her staff to keep the villagers at bay.

Elenna helped Tom to his feet. "Are you hurt?"

Tom shook his head. "I'll be fine. We've wasted enough time here. Let's find the starleaf."

The murmuring voices around them fell silent. Tom looked up and saw hostile faces watching him.

Ched pushed his way to the front of the group, his eyes as hard as flint. "Starleaf? I thought you were here to look into the rockfalls?"

Tom glanced to Elenna – but this time she gave a helpless shrug.

"It's complicated," Tom said. "We think the starleaf and the rockfalls are connected."

Ched snatched up a hammer from the blacksmith's stall, and

brandished it at Tom. "We know
they're connected," Ched snarled.
"The starleaf growing up there on
the Murmuring Peak…" He motioned
to the mountain above the village.
"It's the only thing keeping us safe.
That rare plant has long been lucky
to our people."

"You lied to us," said Selima. She had an axe in her hands.

"You will not get anywhere near our starleaf," said Ched.

Tom took a deep breath and stepped forward. "We may not have told you the full truth," he said loudly and clearly, "but we are still servants of King Hugo. Please, you must trust us."

He hoped the villagers would back down. Some of them were looking at the ground, unsure of themselves, but Ched only sneered.

"We trust nobody. And you're a long way from the palace, young ones." His threat hung in the air.

As the villagers' faces turned ugly, Tom knew Ched was right.

THE MURMURING PEAK

The crowd closed in, weapons clutched in their fists.

We must be outnumbered twenty to one, thought Tom. There was only one way out. He glanced at Elenna, and knew she was thinking the same thing as him.

"Now!" he cried, leaping for Storm's reins and swinging himself into the saddle. Elenna vaulted up behind him. With a kick, Tom sent the stallion charging straight at Ched. The village leader jumped aside, unable to swing his hammer.

"Seize them!" bellowed Ched.

Storm leaped over a market cart and thundered across the square. A few villagers tried to grab his reins, but he was too quick and powerful to be stopped. Stones whizzed past Tom's ears, but soon Storm was carrying them away from the village along a mountain track.

"Something tells me they don't like strangers," said Elenna, when they were at a safe distance.

"Kensa's probably poisoned their thoughts against us," said Tom. "Who knows how long she was waiting for us there?"

They lurched as Storm stumbled to a stop, giving a pained whinny. Tom looked down and saw blood oozing from a gash at the top of his leg.

"A stone must have hit him," said Tom, sliding to the ground.

Elenna dismounted too. "It doesn't

look too bad," she said, inspecting the wound. "I have some herbs that will help."

Tom took out his map. By his reckoning, the Murmuring Peak was the mountain that was rising steeply above them. Somewhere, up there, was a Beast under Kensa's thrall. "I'll make the climb alone," he said.

"Are you sure?" said Elenna.

Tom nodded. "You stay here and look after Storm." He paused. "And if I don't make it back, continue the Quest without me."

Tom set off up the mountainside.

At first the going was hard, but not treacherous. Raffkor's tremors had loosened the rocks, so each time Tom put his foot higher it slid backwards a little. But then it became steeper. Tom rested his hands on the slope and looked upwards. He thought he made out a safe route, where the rock looked firmest, and reached up with his hands. He heaved himself upwards, feeling the burn in his shoulders. *If I fall, at least I'll be protected by Arcta's eagle feath—*

CRACK!

The rock crumbled away.

Oh, no! I gave the feather to Wilfred!

A sickly feeling of dread came over Tom as he looked down. If he lost his grip now, he was dead.

I can't turn back…Vedra is relying on me.

He was panting as he found safe points for his toes in a narrow crack.

The gusts whistled off the peak like whispering voices. *No wonder they call it the Murmuring Peak,* he thought.

Pressing on, he chose his path with extra care. The wind teased at his clothes, threatening to pull him to his death.

Tom was glad to reach a narrow ledge where he could rest. Breathing hard, he looked back and spied Elenna, just a small dot far below.

You'll never succeed, boomed a loud voice.

Tom almost lost his footing. "That was no wind!" he muttered.

Vedra will fall into my mistress's power. Then all your Good Beasts will follow.

Tom realised the voice was coming through the red jewel in his belt.

"Raffkor," he muttered.

Give up, said the voice in his head. *You're no match for me.*

Tom reached for the next handhold. "I'm a match for any Beast!" he hissed.

A crunching sound made him glance up. The rock shook under his fingertips and deadly chips of stone rained down. Tom pressed himself against the rock face and felt the rush of debris fall past. *So Raffkor's waiting for me up there. If I even make it, that is.*

He continued to climb, trying to ignore the thought of what awaited him. Raffkor stamped again further

up the mountain, and more stone
cascaded down.

*You could only just handle me
back in Rion,* said Raffkor's voice.
I'm ten times stronger now.

Tom recalled training with Raffkor
under Wilfred's watchful eye on
a previous Quest. It was true that

the bull-Beast had been a fearsome creature. *We were just playing then,* he said in his mind, sending his thoughts to the Beast. *This time, we fight for real.*

Tom peered up. Ten arm-lengths separated him from the next ledge. And standing on the ledge above that was the muscular blue body of Raffkor.

Three of his horns shone with blue light, the source of his power. The fourth was blackened, just as Vedra's belly had been. He, too, had been poisoned with lunar blood.

The Beast snorted, and swung his massive head.

I'm waiting for you, Tom, he said.

BATTLE ON THE LEDGE

Tom heaved himself onto the first ledge. His arms were trembling from the climb, but he tried not to let the pain show in his face.

Raffkor raked one hoof along the ground above Tom, his flanks rising and falling with rapid breaths. Tom felt his stomach twist in fear. Raffkor was at least twice as large as when

they'd last met. The bull's face wore a
wild, mad stare, his nostrils flaring as
drool spilled from his black lips. Back

in Rion, Raffkor had been unruly, but good natured. Now his snorting breath and heaving flanks seemed full of hate.

The Beast lowered his head, aiming his horns. The black one gave Tom an idea. *Perhaps that's the answer,* he thought, remembering Vedra's black burn. *If I can slice off the blackened horn, maybe that will free Raffkor from Kensa's Evil enchantment.*

With a furious snort, Raffkor leaped down from his ledge. He landed with a bone-shuddering crunch. Tom raised his shield and drew his sword.

Raffkor towered over him. The blue swirls of light that sheathed his horns glowed brighter.

"I know your heart is Good," Tom said clearly.

The bull-Beast tossed his head angrily and stalked forward.

"Remember when we fought side by side, in Rion?" Tom called, trying to remind the Beast.

Raffkor bellowed, lashing his tail like a whip.

"Kensa is not your friend," Tom said. "She's Evil!"

Raffkor let out a snort of fury and charged, covering the ground between them in a flash. Tom scrambled away, using the power of the amber jewel to guide his sword in a defensive slash. The Beast's hot breath blasted his face. Raffkor stopped, then lunged once more.

Tom's foot slipped away from beneath him, and he threw himself against the cliff face. His skin went cold as he peered over the abyss.

I almost fell...

The ledge was only just wide enough for Tom. Raffkor dared not come any closer. Instead, he took two steps back, and stamped his hooves angrily.

Tom clung to the rocks. "While there's blood in my veins," he said, "you'll have to do better than that!"

Raffkor lowered his head. His horns flared and Tom raised his shield just in time. A bolt of blue fire sizzled over the wooden surface. Tom's shield grew so hot that it burned his skin. Blisters started to bulge and the pain was too much to bear. He flung the shield away, watching with horror as his only protection spiralled into the nothingness below. He was too far from the Beast to use his sword.

Prepare to die, boomed Raffkor's voice in Tom's head.

He fired another blast. This time Tom slashed with his sword. The blade deflected the blue bolt and sent it sizzling back towards the Beast. Raffkor lurched aside in panic as the fire cut a gash in the cliff wall.

The Beast's glowing eyes watched Tom intently. *He doesn't dare use his magic again,* thought Tom, *in case it deflects back and strikes him. But there's no way I can get close to him either. It's a stalemate. Unless...*

Tom called out to the bull-Beast, goading him: "Kensa should never have chosen such a weak Beast to defend the starleaf." He faked a mocking laugh. "Fighting you is a waste of my time."

The blue glow was building in the Beast's horns. *He's getting ready to unleash a huge bolt,* thought Tom. *Just what I need.*

Raffkor roared and fired a blinding flash of blue light. Tom swung his sword to meet it. His arms shook as his blade sent the power scorching back at the Beast.

Blue rays exploded on Raffkor's head as the bolt slammed between his eyes. He toppled sideways with a crash.

This is my chance! Tom leaped

forward. Raffkor wouldn't be
stunned for long. The Beast began
to find his feet again, bellowing in
fury and pain, but Tom was bringing
his blade down on the base of the
blackened horn.

Shockwaves shot up Tom's arm as
the steel lodged halfway through the
horn. Black gore spurted from the cut.

Raffkor tossed his massive head and Tom heaved his sword free. The Beast batted at the rocks with his hooves. Tom stepped back and swung again.

This time the blade sheared clean through the horn.

Raffkor's roars shook the mountainside. As the black horn fell down into the abyss below, Tom scrambled back to avoid being smashed in the chest.

It hasn't worked!

Tom didn't know what to do. He couldn't kill a Good Beast, but he had to defend himself.

Raffkor's eyes rolled back, showing just the whites. Then he charged.

Tom had no choice. He raised his sword, aiming it at the Beast's heart.

10

FINDING THE STARLEAF

Raffkor skidded to a halt, close
enough that Tom could smell the
lingering stench of Evil. The Beast's
sides rose in a deep breath, but his
eyes were still and calm. His nostrils
no longer blasted gouts of steam.
The Beast's legs trembled as the
sweat dried in his matted fur, and he
lowered his head.

121

Through the red jewel in his belt,
Tom heard a voice filled with shame.

I am sorry, Master of the Beasts.

Tom's racing pulse began to beat
more slowly. Now he sensed only
Good in the Beast before him.
Slowly, he lowered his sword, then
slid it into its sheath. He held out
a hand and touched Raffkor's head
where the black horn had been.

"There is nothing to be sorry for,"
he said. "You were under Kensa's
Evil enchantment."

You saved me, came back Raffkor's
message. *You took away the Evil
in my body.* So Tom's actions had
worked, after all! Slicing off the
black horn had been the right thing
to do – but only just in time. A

moment later, and Tom would have been lying in a pool of his own blood.

He felt a wave of anger from the Beast, as if Raffkor was remembering his encounter with the cruel sorceress, Kensa.

Tom focused, willing a message to the Beast. *If you really want to get your own back on Kensa, help me find the starleaf.*

Raffkor sank to the ground, lying flat. *Climb on,* he said.

Tom gripped the tuft of hair at the base of Raffkor's neck, and hauled himself onto the broad back. The huge body rocked beneath him as the Beast lumbered to a standing position, his flank muscles rippling.

With a lurch, Raffkor leaped to the

ledge above, hooves crushing stone. Then he began to run, sure-footed, along the narrow ridge.

Tom tried not to look down. This was so different from sitting in Storm's saddle. Each bone-crunching step almost shook him loose.

Soon they reached a plateau right on the top of the Murmuring Peak, and Raffkor paused. Tom looked around. Clouds whipped past, giving everything a ghostly appearance.

A voice drifted up from far below. Not the winds this time, but Elenna.

"Tom? Are you all right?"

Tom cupped his hands to his mouth. "I'm fine!" he called. "And so is Raffkor! We're going to find the starleaf now."

As the clouds cleared, Tom gazed in every direction at the mountains spread out around them. *Avantia looks so peaceful from up here –*

*though nothing could be further
from the truth.*

Among the barren rocks, his
eyes fell on a few green sprigs.
"The starleaf!" he cried, sliding off
Raffkor's back.

Tom approached one of the plants.
Its broad, stiff leaves were shaped
into five points and covered in a fine
fur. A fierce wind ripped across the
mountain top, chilling Tom's skin. As
he turned his head from the gale, his
breath caught in his throat.

"Your horn!" he said, gladly. "It's
grown back!"

Raffkor, untroubled by the freezing
gusts, grunted and tossed his head.
A new blue horn had replaced the
severed black one – Tom was thrilled

to see that the Good Beast was whole again!

Tom kneeled on the ground and gently prised a starleaf root from the earth. He placed it carefully in the satchel Daltec had given him.

"One ingredient down, three to go," he muttered.

As he stood, he realised he was alone. Raffkor had vanished. Tom fought down a feeling of panic. Touching the red jewel in his belt, he felt nothing of Raffkor's presence. Had the huge Beast somehow been blown over the edge? Was that possible?

"Do not worry," said a voice.

Tom spun around and saw Daltec walking towards him. Despite the

gusts, his robes didn't move at all.
He's not really here, Tom reminded
himself. *He's just a vision.*

A scattering of stones made them

both turn around. Tom saw a hand reach over the lip of the mountain top, following by Elenna's dusty face. She brushed herself down as she stood up.

"Quite a climb!" she said. "I didn't want you to have all the fun..." She stopped as she saw the wizard. "Oh, hello, Daltec! Where's Raffkor?"

"Raffkor is safe," said Daltec. "Now you've freed him from the curse, he has come of age. He will be sent to a distant kingdom where he is needed."

"And how is Vedra?" Tom asked.

Daltec face was grim. "The sickness is spreading all the time," he said. Then he nodded to Tom's satchel. "But you have done well to get this far, and find the starleaf."

"I won't give up," said Tom, "but first I need to find my shield."

"I can help with that," said Daltec. The young wizard clicked his fingers, and Tom's shield appeared, floating in the air just in front of him. Tom took it, grateful for the familiar weight on his arm. The surface had a few new scratches, but the tokens were all intact.

"What will happen to all the homeless people?" asked Elenna. "Raffkor destroyed whole villages."

Daltec smiled. "King Hugo is already sending soldiers to help rebuild," he said. "They should be here in a day or two."

"And we need to find Kensa!" said Tom. "She managed to escape."

Daltec shook his head. "Her day of reckoning will come. Your next Quest lies in the Ruby Desert – that's where you'll find the elixir's next ingredient. Those boiling sands will test your endurance and your courage."

"I'm ready," said Tom.

"Kensa will no doubt have sent another corrupted Beast," said Daltec.

"That sorceress can poison as many Good Beasts as she likes," said Tom. "While there's blood in my veins, she will not prevail."

Daltec smiled uneasily. "A new Quest awaits you both."

"We're up to it," Elenna said, grinning broadly.

Tom would never stop being glad to have her by his side.

With the wizard's form hovering nearby, and the starleaf safely tucked away, Tom felt a new sense of hope as he descended the Murmuring Peak with Elenna. The task ahead was daunting – almost impossible – but he promised himself he would keep going until the Beast Quest was complete.

Or until it claimed his life.

THE END

CONGRATULATIONS, YOU HAVE COMPLETED THIS QUEST!

At the end of each chapter you were
awarded a special gold coin.
The QUEST in this book was
worth an amazing11 coins.

Look at the Beast Quest totem picture
on the page opposite to see how far you've
come in your journey to become

MASTER OF THE BEASTS.

The more books you read,
the more coins you will collect!

Do you want your own
Beast Quest Totem?
1. Cut out and collect the coin below
2. Go to the Beast Quest website
3. Download and print out your totem
4. Add your coin to the totem
www.beastquest.co.uk/totem

READ THE BOOKS, COLLECT THE COINS!
EARN COINS FOR EVERY CHAPTER YOU READ!

550+ COINS
**MASTER OF
THE BEASTS**

410 COINS
HERO

350 COINS
WARRIOR

230 COINS
KNIGHT

180 COINS
SQUIRE

44 COINS
PAGE

8 COINS
APPRENTICE

550+
515
480
445
410
395
380
365
350
320
290
260
230
206
191
180
146
112
78
44
30
8

Don't miss the next exciting Beast Quest book in this series, VISLAK THE SLITHERING SERPENT! Read on for a sneak peek...

CHAPTER ONE

OUT OF TIME

The wind buffeted Tom as he climbed down the mountain. It tugged at his hair and clothes and snatched the breath from his throat. He reached for another foothold, and eased himself downwards. He had climbed up the peak to release Raffkor the bull-Beast from Kensa's evil enchantment. Now that Raffkor was free, the next part of Tom's Quest awaited him.

Tom craned his neck to look down. Elenna was climbing down too, just above him, and below stood Silver, her wolf, and Storm, Tom's stallion.

When he reached the bottom, he shook out his aching arms.

Storm trotted to his side and Silver pressed his warm nose into Tom's palm. Tom smiled and stroked the animals' coats.

"I'm so glad that Raffkor is free from Kensa's enchantment," Tom said to Elenna. "I had to cut off his black horn to do it. But another grew back."

"And you found the starleaf for Vedra's cure," Elenna said, grinning.

Tom flipped open his leather satchel. The small five-pointed plant inside looked as fresh as when he had picked it at the top of the peak.

Elenna squared her shoulders. "Now we just need three more ingredients to make the elixir to save Vedra," she said.

"Let's hope we can get them in time," Tom said. He looked up. The moon was a white crescent against the pale blue sky. Tom frowned. It was growing by the day. They had to be back in Avantia's capital city before the full moon, with all four ingredients. If they failed, there would be no cure for Vedra the green dragon, suffering under Kensa's spell. Without a cure, the Good Beast would be lost to the witch's Evil for ever.

Elenna's hand fell on his shoulder. "We'll do it," she said.

Tom nodded. "We have to. But the ingredients are scattered to the corners of the kingdom and guarded by Kensa's enchanted Beasts. We don't have a moment to lose."

"Tom! Elenna!" Tom turned to see Wilfred the Beast Keeper trotting towards them on Breeze, Arcta's golden-brown feather bobbing in his hand.

"You're back!" Wilfred cried. "I knew you'd do it." He held out

Arcta's feather to Tom. "You'd better take this back. I've had enough adventures to last me a lifetime!"

Elenna smiled. "We couldn't have saved Raffkor without you," she said, "but you should get back to the palace and give King Hugo the news."

Tom nodded. He pointed towards a winding path that disappeared over the horizon. "If you follow that road," he said, "it will take you home. But it will be many days' travel."

"I'll take Wilfred to the palace," a cheerful voice said from behind them. Tom turned to see Daltec's smiling face.

"Daltec!" Wilfred started towards the young wizard. "How is Vedra?"

Daltec's smile faded. He looked down at the dusty ground. When he raised his eyes, they were grave. "More and more of his scales have turned black," he said. "It is as Aduro feared. By the next full moon Kensa's lunar blood potion will have taken hold. Vedra will be lost to Evil completely."

Wilfred swallowed. "Send me to him," he said. "I should be at his side."

Daltec nodded, then clicked his fingers. Wilfred and Breeze vanished.

"We must leave too," Tom said. He reached into Storm's saddlebag and pulled out his magic map. Near the bottom, a deep red glow pulsed steadily. A word appeared.

VISLAK.

Tom nodded slowly. He had met Vislak once before. He was a mighty Beast, a great red snake as tall and thick as an oak tree. Now Vislak was cursed, he would be a fearsome enemy. Tom turned the map towards Daltec and Elenna.

"Look," Tom said, pointing at the red area on the map. "Our next Quest lies at the edge of the Ruby Desert. It looks at least six days' travel." He glanced again at the waxing moon, frustration welling inside him. "We don't have time!" he said.

"No," Daltec said, "and I can't magic you all that far."

"Then we only have one option," said Elenna. "We need the help of a flying Beast."

Read
VISLAK THE SLITHERING
SERPENT
to find out more!